To Codi Josephson, for friendship and for the story of
the boy. To Keshunyah Chambers, for the half moon.
And to menders everywhere, who love their families,
their neighborhoods, and their libraries.
—M.E.


Dedicated to the common thread of sibling love and the
ties that bind them together. Inspired by my own little
Zora and Lee—my grandchildren, Indya and Myles.
—A.H.

Text copyright © 2022 by Michelle Edwards
Jacket art and interior illustrations copyright © 2022 by April Harrison

All rights reserved. Published in the United States by Anne Schwartz Books, an imprint of Random House
Children's Books, a division of Penguin Random House LLC, New York.
Anne Schwartz Books and the colophon are trademarks of Penguin Random House LLC.

Visit us on the Web! rhcbooks.com
Educators and librarians, for a variety of teaching tools,
visit us at RHTeachersLibrarians.com

Library of Congress Cataloging-in-Publication Data is available upon request.

ISBN 978-0-593-31067-0 (trade) — ISBN 978-0-593-31068-7 (lib. bdg.) — ISBN 978-0-593-31069-4 (ebook)

The text of this book is set in 15-point Meta Pro Book.
The illustrations were rendered in collage, acrylic, artist pens, and pencils.
Book design by Sarah Hokanson

MANUFACTURED IN CHINA
10 9 8 7 6 5 4 3 2 1 First Edition

# ME AND THE BOSS

## A Story About Mending and Love

# Michelle Edwards & April Harrison

a·s·b

anne schwartz books

I know big sisters. Zora, the boss,
she's mine. I go wherever she goes,
and we are always home before dark.
Those are the rules.

"Hurry up," orders the boss, and we race all the way to the library. Inside the heavy wooden doors . . .

I follow Zora past the computers
and the shelves of books...

and into a room of big kids.

The teacher tells us to call her Mrs. C. She gives everyone but me threads. Also, a needle with a big eye and a sharp point, like a tiger's tooth. She thinks I am a baby, not old enough for a sharp tiger's tooth.

"Lee needs one," says Zora. Everyone listens to the boss. "He looks small, but he is really eight."

Am not. Not even seven yet.

I sit tall. Mrs. C gives me my own stuff.

"Thank you," I say before the boss tells me to, because I am polite on my own.

Mrs. C shows us how to sail our thread through the needle's eye like a little boat. She shows us how to slip our needle in and slide it out to make a stitch. She shows us how our stitches can make a picture. Then she gives us cloth squares so we can embroider, too.

Right away my needle and my thread
boat hit my finger and sting it like a bee.
"Take your time, Lee." Mrs. C helps me
stitch slow till others need her help.

Alone, I poke and jab, jab and poke.

The boss makes a fine flower.

"What's that?"
She points at mine.

"A half-moon," I tell her, but Zora isn't really listening.
She is busy stitching.

I look at my jumble
of threads. I am done.
I reach into my pocket
and there's a hole
where my quartz
rock used to be.
I dig deeper and the
hole gets bigger.
   "Stop squirming,"
the boss orders. "I
need to finish my leaf."

Outside the windows, the sky is not bright anymore.
It is time to go.

"You can take your work home, like this." Mrs. C
rolls a needle and threads inside a cloth. I do that and
put mine deep in my good pocket.

In the near dark, me and Zora are long shadows. We stick together. She walks fast, and I walk fast, too. I reach for her hand, and she squeezes mine.

At home, the boss shows off her flower.
"Pretty," Mom says.
"Wow!" Dad says.
Now they want to see what I made.
"It's a surprise," I say. I don't want them to see my mess. Not yet.

Later in my room, I snuggle with Mom as she reads me to sleep. I keep my needle and threads and half-moon hidden.

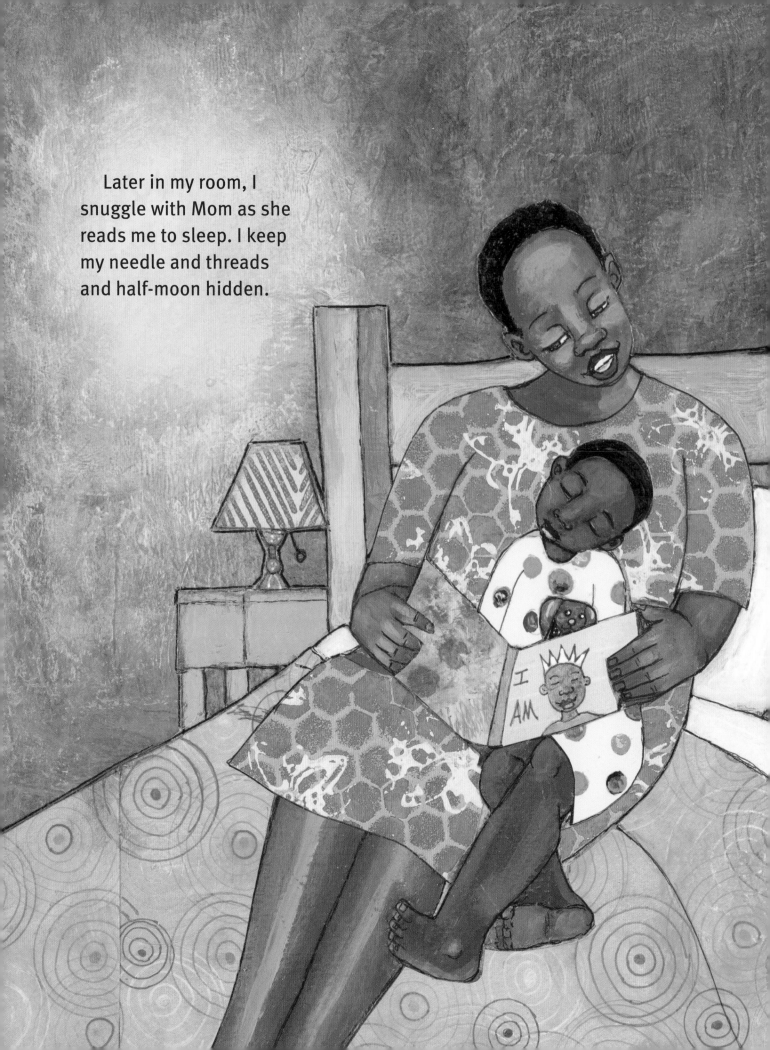

In the deepest night, a screechy loud wakes me.

I can't get back to sleep, so I turn on my little light. I dig out my
cloth bundle and unroll it. Everything is still there, waiting for me.

With my needle, I poke a stitch and
snag my hurt finger. I quick brave another.
    That tiger's tooth, mean and sharp,
catches me again.
    Take your time, Lee.

I look at my hands.
Slow down, I tell them,
and after a few stitches,
they start to listen!

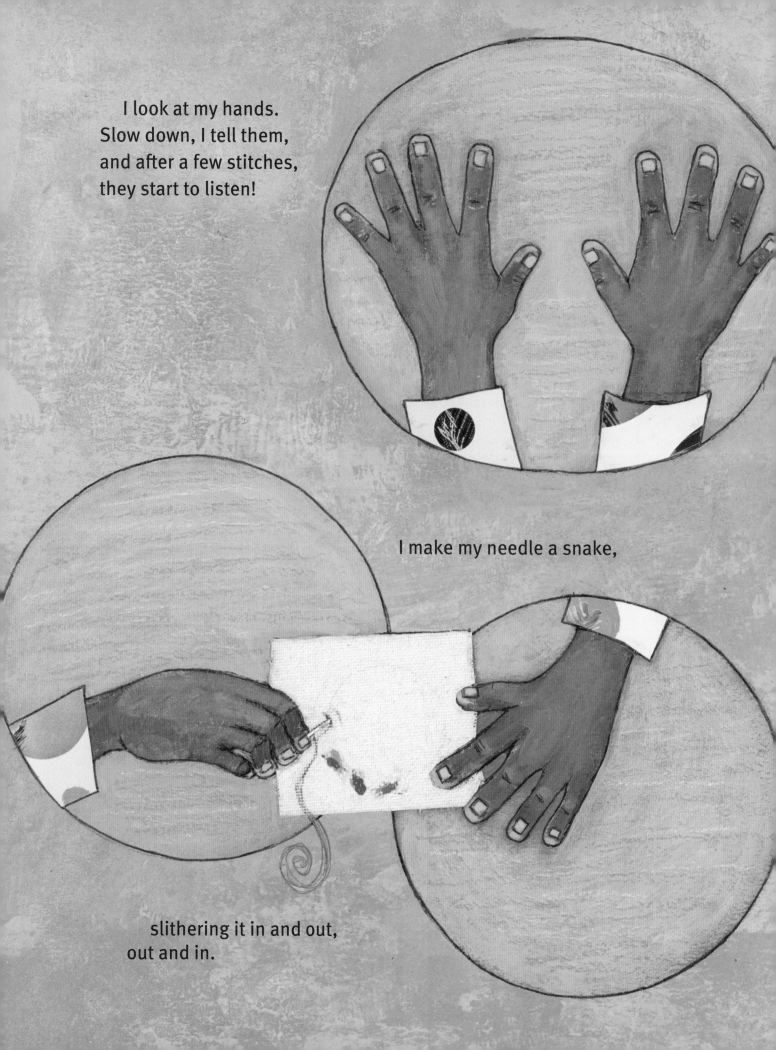

I make my needle a snake,

slithering it in and out,
out and in.

Slowly, my moon
grows fuller . . .

and fuller . . .

and full!

When I give my moon a smile,
a little wheel turns inside my
head, and I smile back. I am not
done yet.

I grab my pants, flip them inside out, and find that hole in the pocket.

I send my needle over and around it, again and again, closing it tight.

The pocket doesn't look perfect, but my finger can't poke through anymore.

A mighty feeling roars through me and fills the night.

I fold my pants over my desk chair. I roll my needle and threads in an old T-shirt and set it, and my moon, on top of my desk. Back in bed, I turn off the little light and sleep finds me.

As soon as morning comes, I sneak into the boss's room while she is eating breakfast.

I sew the ear back on Bess, her bear, then I rush to the kitchen.

"Look," I say proudly. I wave my smiling moon at the boss. I show off my pocket. Then I hand her Bess.

Zora looks. She checks all my stitches. She tugs on her bear's ear. It stays on!

"You!" She wraps me and Bess in her special hug, and we share something that is bigger than my pocket, bigger than Bess's ear, maybe even bigger than me or Zora.

When it's our time to go to the park,
"Get ready!" Zora orders. I fixed her bear,
and she's back to being the boss.

I grab my jacket, put my moon in my mended pocket, and follow her out the door.

# How to Make Lee's Smiling Moon
### by Michelle Edwards and Alisa Weinstein

Lee embroidered a smiling moon. Why don't you try to embroider one, too?

FABRIC: 6-inch square of cotton cloth

NEEDLE: Embroidery needle

THREAD: Embroidery floss

NOTIONS: Water-soluble fabric marker, scissors, measuring tape

Here are the instructions:

- *An adult can help you measure and cut your cloth square and piece of embroidery floss. They can also help you thread your needle and tie a knot.*

- Using a water-soluble fabric marker, draw a moon on your cloth. Don't forget the smile!

- Cut a piece of embroidery floss the length of the distance between your hand and your shoulder.

- Thread the floss through the eye of your needle and tie a knot at the other end.

- Do a running stitch, poking up and pulling, poking down and pulling, following along your drawn moon. It will look like a dotted line.

- Keep making stitches, poking up and pulling, poking down and pulling, until your moon is done.

- Knot your floss close to the cloth, and snip.

- Your moon is done!